Narcisse-Eutrope Dionne

John and Sebastian Cabot

Narcisse-Eutrope Dionne

John and Sebastian Cabot

ISBN/EAN: 9783337399269

Printed in Europe, USA, Canada, Australia, Japan

Cover: Foto ©Andreas Hilbeck / pixelio.de

More available books at **www.hansebooks.com**

CABOT

JOHN AND SEBASTIAN

CABOT

BY

N. E. DIONNE

LIBRARIAN OF THE LEGISLATIVE LIBRARY OF THE
PROVINCE OF QUEBEC

QUEBEC
RAOUL RENAULT, PUBLISHER

—

1898

JOHN AND SEBASTIAN

CABOT

—

I

JOHN CABOT, generally known as the discoverer of North America, was not a Venetian by birth, as some writers say, but a Genoese. In fact, he had been naturalized as a Venetian, in consequence of a residence of fifteen years, by a unanimous vote of the Senate of Venice, on the 28th March, 1476. Some writers presume that he was born at Castiglione, in Liguria, others say Chioggia, one of the

5

lagoon islands, but these two assertions are based upon documents of no value. Dr Puebla, the ambassador of Ferdinand and Isabella to England, also Pedro de Ayala, Puebla's adjunct in the embassy, write that Cabot was a Genoese by birth.

John Cabot was married to a Venetian woman, who followed him to England, and we find it recorded that on the 27th of August, 1497, she was living at Bristol, England, with her children Lewis, Sebastian and Sanctus. At that time they were apparently all of age, Sebastian having attained at least the age of twenty-three. Sebastian, therefore, was born in 1474. According to certain English biographers, Sebastian Cabot's native place was England ; this statement carries but little weight, as it seems pretty sure that he was born in Venice. When his father was naturalized a Venetian in 1476, as already stated, in consequence of a constant residence of fifteen years in Venice, Sebastian must have then been not less than two years old. Many authors say that he was a Venetian, specially Ramusio, Andrea Navajero, Contarini, Oviedo, Peter Martyr, etc.

We are inclined to believe that John Cabot removed from Venice to England in 1490, and previous to that he visited Portugal and Spain to obtain royal aid to undertake transatlantic discoveries. He also visited Mecca, where he met caravans bringing spices from afar. He believed in the sphericity of the earth, and inferred from their replies that these spices came originally from the West, whence his project of finding a maritime and shorter route to Cathay.

In the year 1496, Cabot obtained letters-patent from Henry VII for a voyage of discovery westward. He left Bristol in the beginning of May, 1497, on a small ship called the *Matthew*, manned by eighteen men. When the vessel had reached the west coast of Ireland, it sailed towards the north, then to the west for seven hundred leagues, and reached the mainland. He then sailed along the coast three hundred leagues. Returning to Bristol, Cabot saw two islands to starboard. This is the summary of his first voyage.

II

CABOT'S FIRST VOYAGE, 1497

On what data is based the affirmation, sustained with amusing boldness, that Cabot's landfall on his first voyage to America is Cape Breton? Is there, in support of this affirmation, any documentary proof worth being quoted? There is a map by Cabot—at least it is thought that the map is his (1)—and nothing else can be found. We will examine it further on. There are also some relations of this voyage which have been cited as proofs of this assertion. Let us examine them, with a view of leaving no put-off to those who might think that I ignored them intentionally, fearing their arguments against the thesis that I wish to set up and defend.

(1) Several historians doubt this, especially Eben Norton Hereford, William Cullen Bryant, Mgr Howley, James P. Howley, Dr Kohl. Justin Winsor does not guarantee its complete authenticity.

Lorenzo Pasqualigo, merchant of London, wrote, on the 23rd August 1497, to his brothers in Venice :

" The Venetian, our countryman, who went with a ship from Bristol, is returned, and says that 700 leagues hence he discovered land in the territory of the Grand Cham. He coasted 300 leagues and landed... Was three months on the voyage... His name is Zuan Cabot... The discoverer planted on his new-found land a large cross, with one flag of England and one of St Mark...

On the following day, August 24, 1497, Raimondo de Soncino, envoy of the Duke of Milan to Henry VII, wrote the following passage in a despatch to his government :

" Also, some months ago, his Majesty sent out a Venetian who is a very good mariner, and has good skill in discovering new islands, and he has returned safe, and has found two very large and fertile new islands, having likewise discovered the Seven Cities, four hundred leagues from England in the western passage."

Some months after, the same Soncino wrote another and a more explicit letter on the Cabots' expedition.

" Having set out from Bristol, and passed the western limits of Hibernia, and then standing to the northward, he began to steer eastward, leaving (after a few days) the North Star on his right hand..."

We do not see anything about Cape Breton in these letters. More fortunate than several others, Cabot had the opportunity of seeing the Seven Cities, four hundred leagues from England. It is evident that, at this time, they were still sailing in the " Dark Sea ".

Peter Martyr d'Anghiera's relation is a little different; but of Cape Breton, not a word :

" Cabot directed his course so farre toward the northe pole, that even in the mooneth of July he fonde monstruous heapes of Ice swimming on the sea, and in maner continuall day lyght. Yet sawe he the lande in that tracte, free from Ise. Thus seyng suche heapes of Ise before hym, he was enforced to tourne his sayles and folowe the weste, so coastyng styll by the shore, that he was thereby broughte so farre into the southe by reason of the lande bendynge so much southwarde that it was there almost equall in latitude with the sea called *Fretum Herculeum*, havynge the north pole elevate in maner in the same degree. He sayled lykewise in this tracte so form towards the weste, that he had the Islande of Cuba on his lefte hande in maner in the same degree of longitude ". (1)

Another anonymous relation, which is attributed to Cabot himself, confirms, in a vague manner, that of Peter Martyr :

_____

(1) Anghiera, *Decad*. iij. book VI, fo. 55.

11

" At the beginning of the year 1496, I began to sail in the north western direction, expecting to come across no other land than Cathay, and pass from thence to India ; but, after some days, I discovered that the land extended towards the tramontane, which disappointed me exceedingly. I however ran along the coast in the hope of finding a gulf. I could sail around. I did not discover any, but I remarked that the land extended as far as the 56th degree of our pole. Seeing that at that place the coast was running towards the East, and giving up all hopes to find the passage, I sailed back with a view of ascertaining again the said coast in the direction of the equator, always with the intention of finding a passage to India; but I arrived at that part now called Florida ". (1)

Let us set aside all the contradictory versions we have found in the relations of Cabot's first voyage, and let us examine in brief what can be made out of the rest.

When leaving England Cabot sailed to the North. Forced by the ice, he must have sailed westward as far as the American coast, he then sailed towards the East to the neighbourhood of Florida. He returned directly to Bristol.

I may add, to complete these details, that Cabot left Bristol on the 2nd of May, 1497, on the *Matthew*, a vessel of a

(1) Ramusio, Raccolta, t. 1, p. 414.

small tonnage, and that on the 6th of August of the same year he was back from his voyage.

Such is the version generally accepted. In fact, it is the only one that has been known until these last years, when some historians, whose respectability is not questioned, have made up their minds to give another interpretation by maintaining that Cabot landed at Cape Breton, at a precise spot, Cape North, and at a precise date which they fixed on the sixth of June, at five o'clock in the morning. And there Cabot planted a cross and hoisted up the colors of St. George and St. Mark. England and Venice, his two countries!

According to the same historians, Cabot would have, on this very same day, extended his exploration south-westward, and in the evening of the 24th of June, he would have come across a large island which he named Island of St. John. This is Prince Edward Island.

We must express our great astonishment at such rapid sailing. We calculate about ninety nautical miles between Cape North and the East point of Prince Edward Island. By allowing fifteen hours of day navigation to the Venetian navigator, he would have headed, on the 24th of June, six miles an hour. But the *Matthew* had only sailed two miles an hour since its departure from Bristol. How can this rapid sailing be satisfactorily explained?

From Bristol to Cape North, the distance is about two thousand two hundred and fifty miles, according to Harrisse. Cabot took fifty-two days to make this passage, from the 2nd of May to the 24th of June. Without stopping anywhere during the passage, he would have sailed forty-three miles per day, that is a little less than two miles an hour. And on the 24th of June, the *Matthew*, newly supplied with wings, would have sailed six miles an hour! I refuse to believe in such a phenomenon.

The greatest probability is that Cabot sailed directly towards Labrador; then, following the West coast of Newfoundland, he directed his course towards Florida, without entering the gulf of St. Lawrence. His famous landfall might reasonably have been Cape *Bonavista*, which has retained part of the appellation *Primavista*, as we can see on Sebastian Cabot's map. Such is the opinion of several distinguished historians, very familiar with this particular historical controversy. Mgr Howley, bishop of St. Johns, is of opinion that the landfall was effected on the Newfoundland coast, and he is not far from believing that the precise point is Cape St. John.

Mr. D. W. Prowse, author of an appreciated history of Newfoundland, also believes that the landfall took place on the Newfoundland coast, and, according to his version, all the probabilities are in favor of Cape Bonavista.

14

Harrisse pleads for Labrador.

According to the same author, all the cosmographers and chart-makers of Charles V, though supplied directly by Sebastian Cabot in his quality of Pilot-Major, supervisor of the Chair of Cosmography in the *Casa de Contratacion*, and member of the commission of pilots and geographers, located the first translatlantic discoveries under the British flag along the region then called Labrador.

Some other writers claim that Cabot has landed at Cape Ann, towards the 42nd degree of north latitude.

Whatever may come of these divers testimonies, it is evident that the contemporary historians do not agree. This divergency is sufficiently accentuated to restrain our historians from going too far in support of their favorite thesis.

III

CABOT'S MAP

If Cabot be the first European who landed on Cape Breton, like all the explorers of his century, he must have given it a name according to the circumstances of the time and place. Now, a Venetian like him, in the service of England, could not think of calling it Cape Breton, which was too French a name for an English man. But England was then named Britannia, proclaimed some time ago, Mr. Gerald E. Hart, in a lecture given at Montreal. An error, a grave error! I have perused several works of the latter end of the fifteenth century, as well as the maps of the first half of the next century, and I could not find anywhere that the inhabitants of the noble and proud Albion were designated by the name of Britons. Everywhere and always they were called *Anglais, English, Ingleses.*

Great Britain, with its actual boundaries, is indicated on the maps by the words *Anglia*, *Scotia*, and Ireland is called *Hibernia. Britannia*, it is France ! If we refer to the maps of the world, the planispheres, and the *portulans*, from Maggiolo's map (1527) to that of Gastaldi in Ramusio (1550), we never fail to find the same designation in regard to Cape Breton.

Verazzano (1528) : *Cap de Bretton.*

Ribero (1529) : *Cap del Breton.*

Münster (1540) : *C. Britonum.*

Ulpins (1542) : *Cavo de Britoni.*

Rotz (1542) : *Cabo Bretos.*

Jean Alfonse (1544–45) : *Cap Breton.*

Vallard (1545) : *C. Breton.*

Henri II (1546) : *Terre des Bretons.*

Freire (1546) : *C. Bretain.*

The map in the British Museum (No. 9814) also bears the same name : *Terra de los Britones.*

But some critics may oppose that Sebastian Cabot's map gives also *del Berto*, and that he may have himself so named it, and that all the cartographers of his time have copied him.

This objection has no value, Cabot's map was drawn in 1544, when really remarkable cosmographical works had been published, for instance that of Ribeiro, this notable map of which a fine copy is kept at the Propaganda. Some historians dispute the authenticity of the Cabotian map and think it is apocryphical. Some have seen in it the hands of some one else than Cabot and without his knowledge. Some others consider it a reliable document, sure, indiscutable and on which we can rely. I do not want to accept the theory of these last mentioned historians.

Therefore, in 1544, Sebastian Cabot drew up the map which was to reveal to the world the numerous and important discoveries his father had made in 1497, forty-three years before, when he himself was but twenty or twenty-three years of age. A thorough perusal of this document discloses some very singular things.

For instance we can see the nomenclature of some places given by Jacques Cartier in 1534 and in 1535. To wit: *la aga de Golesma*, for the lake d'Angoulême (Saint-Pierre), *Rio de S. Quenain* for the Saguenay River, *Rio de Fouez* for the River Fouez (St. Maurice) Brest, the Islands Bay. How can these French names be explained in a satisfactory manner, on the Cabotian map. Where did Cabot get them? No one will dare to advance that he had collected his informations in one of his late voyages, or that he or his father had traced them in

19

the sketches done during their first expedition to America. It would be wiser to say that Cabot unscrupulously took his information from the maps published before his, such as Cartier's map, the Dauphin's or that of Henri II, which, according to Dr. Kohl and d'Avezac, was copied in 1542 on or about that time. He must have also especially consulted the map of Nicolas Desliens, which was drawn at Dieppe, in 1541, one copy of which can be found in the Royal Library of Dresden. The configuration is very near identical, to such an extent that, when comparing them together, we cannot but exclaim that one has copied the other. Therefore, as Desliens' planisphere preceded Cabot's map, it is only just to presume that Cabot is his humble and servile imitator, to say the least. This last fact, reported by Harrisse, is, for us, very conclusive. No one, that I know, has opposed any refutation to that argument relative to the value of the Cabotian map. Not only the configuration is the same, but the same nomenclature of places can be found with a designation and an orthography that would lead us to believe that the same man is the author of both. In any case, if there be some divergency, it is not apparent enough to destroy the belief that one ignored the other.

Here is what Mgr Howley says about the famous Cabot map :

" Whatever may be thought of the authenticity of the map

as a whole, there can be no doubt that the words *Prima vista* are the work of a later hand. They are printed in large, square and most conspicuous characters, entirely different from any thing else on the map. But not content with this, the author (or interpolater) repeats the words in the following manner: " *Prima terra vista* " marking the same spot. Here, again, are signs of tampering, for these words are in Italian, while all the rest of the map (with two remarkable exceptions) is in Spanish, etc."

How could Cabot give such a faithful delineation of the river St. Lawrence, when it is known that he never visited its shores? Where has he become aware of the existence of the lake d'Angoulême, of the River de Fouez and other places discovered and named by Jacques Cartier?

It is very probable that the relations of the voyages of the *Discoverer* of Canada, written before 1540, that his marine map, of which Jacques Noël, one of his inheritors and descendants deplored the disappearance, in 1587, as well as the cartographical works of Pierre Desliens and of Roberval's pilot, have been largely used by all the cartographers of the latter part of the sixteenth century and even by Cabot. This army of geographers who invaded the European Courts at that period of discoveries could not know anything by themselves of the American continent and especially of the new found lands.

21

Who will pretend, now, that Gastaldi, Ortelius, Wytfliet, Cornelius de Jode and nearly all the other cartographers have taken their compass and pen after having previously visited the places they wanted to describe? They have merely sought for their information from one another, they have servilely copied one another, and they have made the very same topographical errors. Cabot had for his information in regard to the new found lands and Canada, the relations of Jacques Cartier, the map of Jean Alphonse, the Dauphin's map, that of Nicolas des Liens, whilst the Dutch and the Spaniards, who came later on, have had the opportunity of modelling their works on those of Vallard, of Cabot himself and on some others who have contributed to spread geographical science.

Harrisse has it as follows :

" The conclusion to be drawn is that Sebastian Cabot's statements as regards the first landfall on the continent of North America are in absolute contradiction to the legends and delineations of the planisphere of 1544, and that these, in their turn, are based entirely on the discoveries made by Jacques Cartier in 1534 and 1536 and not at all on Cabot's."

IV

THE LANDFALL

Here is the gordian knot. The difficulty effectively lies in the famous inscription which can be seen on Cabot's map, at the North extremity of Cape Breton, near the spot now called Cape North :

PRIMA TIERRA VISTA, or, *the first land seen.* This land, says the explanatory legend of the map, was discovered by Joan Caboto, a Venetian, and Sebastian Caboto, his son, in the year of Our Lord MCCCCXCIIII, the twenty-fourth of June in the morning ; they called it by the name of *prima tierra vista,* and to a large island in the neighborhood of the said land the name of Saint Joan was given, it having been discovered on the day of the feast of Saint John.

23

So the Cabotian map says. The first land seen when he reaches America is Cape Breton. It was, we must remember the date well, on the 24th June 1494 !

This land was called by Cabot *Prima tierra vista !*

The same day, he discovers the Island of St. John !

Evidently, Cabot, junior, had already, in 1544, lost his memory, for he puts his voyage three years back. It is no more 1497, but 1494. Some writers have tried to explain this anachronism by attributing it to an error of the engraver. Explanations of that kind are always unsatisfactory, and we are not bound to accept them. I would rather believe that it is the cartographer or the translator who has committed that error, the more so if his name was not Sebastian Cabot. Harrisse says appropriately : " The critic has then the right of asking if that document, of which only one copy is known to-day, has not undergone during the course of years, the fate peculiar to documents of the same kind, and if the copy in the Bibliothèque Nationale gives a representation of the original type, similar in all its parts to that made out by Sebastian Cabot ".

According to Harrisse, there had been four editions of that map :

1. The map in the Bibliothèque Nationale, drawn in 1544 ; found at a curate's dwelling in Bavière in 1843 ;

2. The map seen at Oxford by Nicolas Heschoff, in 1666 ; drawn in 1549 ;

3. The map engraved by Clement Adams, seen by Hakluyt in 1565 ;

4. Finally the map Purchas pretends to have examined in the private gallery of the King of England. It bore the date of 1549.

All these editions are quite alike, but they all differ on several points. Without losing our time by making tedious comparisons, we may say, in brief, that the Cabotian map is far from being a document on which we can rely to make assertions in matters of discoveries, and still more so in geographical science. In certain respects, the learned professor of cosmography is far behind others. Newfoundland is, according to him, but a vast archipelago ; Cape Breton is a main land, etc., etc. The French maps issued before his are, generally, more accurate.

The map drawn by Sebastian Cabot is the only one which claims, by its legend, that the English have been the first to land at Cape Breton. All the other geographical monuments of that period do not say a word about it. However, they are unanimous in limiting the English discoveries to Labrador. Let us make a short analysis of those old maps.

The map of Juan de la Cosa, drawn in 1500, shows us the *Cavo de Inglaterra* (cape of England) ; Humboldt believes it to be a promontory in the neighborhood of Belle-Isle, which would now be, according to Dr Kohl, Cape Race.

It is the remotest mention of English discoveries, and it belongs to Newfoundland. We are still far from Cape Breton.

In 1511 a *portulan* was published by the Vicomto de Maggiolo. M. D'Avezac describes it as follows :

" The polar regions in a radius of nearly thirty-five degrees offer the most curious and singular configurations surrounding the Polar sea, with a continuous cloud from the *Norvega* to one *Terra de los Ingress* (English Land), more to the North by about ten degrees than the *Terra de Lavorador de rey de portugall* ".

It is now more to the North that we must look for Cabot's discoveries.

The map of Robert Thorne (1527), an Englishman of Bristol, places parallel to Labrador which he calls *Nova terra laboratorum dicta*, the following legend : *Terra nec ab Anglis primum fuit inventa*, that is : LAND FIRST DISCOVERED BY THE ENGLISH.

We can read on Ribeiro's map where Labrador should be : *Esta tierra descubrieron los Ingleses*, or, THIS LAND HAS BEEN DISCOVERED BY THE ENGLISH.

Verazzano's map marks out Labrador with this legend :

Questra terra fu discoperta da inghilesi, with the arms of England over it.

Wolfenbuttel's globe (1534) is more explicit than the others. At Labrador we can read this legend : *Ce pays fut découvert par les Anglais de la ville de Bristol*, that is : THIS COUNTRY WAS DISCOVERED BY THE ENGLISH OF THE CITY OF BRISTOL. Now, when Cabot left his country, he settled at Bristol. There can be no question of some other discoverers.

From 1534, the cartographers seem to have forgotten all about Cabot's voyages. They only pay attention to the discoveries of Jacques Cartier and Jean Alfonse, Roberval's pilot, and they distort all their geographical and hydrographical data. It seems that Cabot's map should have brought some new documents to the map makers. But the scientific men have only been aware of his landing in an approximate manner and they are unanimous in placing it in the Labrador regions.

If we look attentively into the opinions of the historians of the latter part of the fifteenth century who have written on the English discoveries in America, we are astonished to find the same confusion which always prevails in all the relations. Like Peter Martyr, Ramusio and Gomara do not mention any date. Some have placed the first voyage in 1494 ; some others in 1496, 1497, 1498 and even 1516.

According to some writers, Cabot landed at Labrador, while others put his landing at Newfoundland. A few are of opinion that he returned to Bristol before landing on the American continent.

As my fixed intention is to prove everything I advance, I will give some authorities, beginning with Peter Martyr, the personal friend of Sebastian Cabot.

" These regions are cauled *Terra Florida* and *Regio Baccalearum* or *Bacchallaos* of the which you may reade sumwhat in this booke in the voyage of the woorthy owlde man yet lyving, Sebastiane Cabote, in the VI booke of the thyrde Decade. But Cabot touched only in the north corner and most barbarous part hereof, from whense he was repulsed with Ise in the moneth of July " (1).

Purchas has left a narration attributed to Cabot himself, in the following terms :

" The map of *Sebastian Cabot*, cut by *Clement Adams*, relateth, That *John Cabot*, a Venetian and his sonne *Sebastian*,

_____

(1) Martyr. The Discoverer of the New World. Preface to the Reader, by Richard Eden.

set out from Bristol, discovering the Land, called it *Prima Vista*, and the Island before it *S. Johns.* " (1)

In the fourth volume of the *Encyclopedia Britannica*, we read the following words :

" This year (1497), on St. John the Baptist's day, the land of America was found by the merchants of Bristowe in a ship of Bristol called the *Matthew*, the which said ship departed from the port of Bristowe, the second of May, and came home again 6th August following ". And in a note at the bottom of the page : " These important dates are from an ancient manuscript for several generations in possession of the family of Hill Court, Gloucestershire. " (2)

But here is a last testimony which is worth its weight in gold. I suppose it has been overlooked by several historians who might have used it with profit. It is that of Ellis, an English writer, whose good faith cannot be suspected. Here is the passage I find in his work entitled : *Voyage to Hudson's Bay :*

" In the Spring of the Year following being 1497, he (John Cabot) sailed from Bristol, with one Ship fitted out at the King's Expence, and three or four smaller Vessels freighted

---

(1) Purchas. His Pilgrimage, London, 1617, p. 915.
(2) Encyclopedia Britannica, vol. 4, p. 350.

by the Merchants there, with coarse Caps, Cloth, Laces, etc., upon his Discovery ; in which upon the 24th of June, about Five in the Morning, he saw Land, which for that Reason he called *Prima Vista*, or, first seen, which was Part of Newfoundland and afterwards another Smaller Island, which he called St. John's ". (1)

Therefore, it is not necessary to refer to Cabot's map to have an idea of the English discovery in America. Ellis seems even more learned than Cabot the cartographer, who, in 1544, had already lost the date of his first voyage. How is it that several of our modern historians are so intent in speaking of the legend of the Cabotian map, with its *Prima Vista*, its Island of St. John, and that they set aside the relation of a man so well informed as Ellis? Is it because they did not read Ellis? If they read him, they prefered not to say a word about what he reports.

Everything can be found in his relation :

The year !—1497.

The date !—The 24th of June.

The hour !—Five o'clock in the morning.

---

(4) *A Voyage to Hudson's Bay, in the years* 1746 and 1747. By Henry Ellis. London, 1748. p. 3-4.

The land discovered !—Newfoundland.

The precise spot !—Prima Vista.

The neighboring island !—St. John.

What more categorical details do we want?

What can be given to contradict this testimony?

Nothing else but Cabot's map, and we know what to think of it.

Apocryphical? Perhaps.

Imperfect? Certainly.

Interpolated? Very probably.

" All these facts prove, says Harrisse, that the names, legends and configurations of the northern extremity of the New Continent, as inscribed and depicted in charts emanating from Spanish cosmographers, in general, and Diego Ribeiro in particular, were supplied directly by Sebastian Cabot or through his professional instrumentality, and that for almost half a century he placed his landfall many degrees farther north than the *Prima vista* of the Cabotian planisphere of 1544." (1)

---

(1) Harrisse. John Cabot, p. 84.

V

GENERAL CONSIDERATIONS

There are some deductions flowing from what has been previously said, that can be invoked against those who believe in the Cabotian map as in a text of the Bible.

1. Is it not strange, at first, that Cabot the cartographer has placed his *Prima Tierra Vista* on the *Terre des Bretons* as it was called later. Cabot had not then seen any land before arriving at Cape Breton? Therefore, what course did he follow? All the historians are unanimous in saying that he coasted the American Continent, some at the 62nd, others at the 58th or 56th degree of North latitude. Consequently, he must have either come across Labrador or Newfoundland. Is it not right to believe that, before entering the gulf of St. Lawrence, if he ever penetrated into it, he coasted the eastern side of the Labrador or Newfoundland territories?

Nevertheless, it is well established that Cabot sailed along the coasts for a length of three hundred leagues before returning.

Hakluyt left us the text of the legend published on Cabot's map, in Clement Adams' edition. It reads as follows :

" In the yeere of our Lord 1494 (read 1497) John Cabot a Venetian...discovered that land which no man before that time had attempted, on the 24 of June, about five of the clocke early in the morning. This land he called Prima Vista, that is to say First seene, because as I suppose it was that part whereof they had the first sight from sea ... "

2. When we know that Cabot had most of the maps published before his, which he had the opportunity of collecting in his quality of pilot major and professor of cosmography in the *Hotel du Négoce* at Seville, how can we explain the strange fact of his placing Cape Breton three degrees more to the South East than the Cape where he puts his famous inscription ? We must conclude that he knew nothing of the geography of these regions.

3. In the documents previously quoted and in some others which were published afterwards, we find, when Cabot's discoveries of new lands are mentioned, the English terms of *New found land* or *New found isle*. What does this mean ?

Barnett wrote in his history of Bristol these significant words : " In the year 1497, June 24th, on Saint John's day, as it is in a manuscript in my possession, was *Newfoundland* found by Bristol men in a ship called the Matthew."

It is no one else than Cabot who is meant by " Bristol men ".

Pasqualigo in his letter dated August 23rd, 1497, says : " The discoverer planted on his *new found land* a large cross ".

On August the 6th, when he arrived from America, Cabot received from Henri VII, as a reward for his services a gratification which has been taken from the royal chest.   It is indicated in the following note : " To him who *found* the *New Isle*, 10 l.

Has any one had the idea of attributing this appellation of *new found land* to another land or island than Newfoundland ? In any case, who has ever thought of Cape Breton ?

4. As to the Island of St. John, Dr Kolh is of opinion that its name has been given by the French, and that Cabot has only, for this, copied the French maps.   This opinion seems to me to be the most admissible.

In Jean Alfonse *Cosmosgraphie*, commenced in 1544 and terminated the 24th of November 1545—Cabot's map was then very little known—we find the *Isle de Saint-Jean* perfectly described, not only in the maps but also in the text of

35

his work. The following passage is remarkable for its accuracy and precision : " If you run twenty leagues to the west north west along the coast, in the center of this region and nearer the Terre de Breton than the new found land... St. Jean and Bryon and Bird Island are at the 47⁰ north. "

Is it not reasonable to believe, when we read this paragraph of his *Cosmographie,* that Jean Alfonse is the first European who called Prince Edward Island by a name which ought to be still in honor. Some one may object that the pilot of Saintonge might have had the opportunity of consulting Cabot's map published in 1544. It is very improbable that Alfonce had seen this map, when Cabot was still working at it, unless he had been in relation with Cabot himself. Cabot was then living at Seville, in Spain, and he could not think of travelling on account of his two charges. If one had the opportunity of having the other's work, it was Cabot, who, on account of his position, was endeavoring to collect all the maps of which he heard.

5. We have already seen that the name of Cape Breton was not given by Cabot. He committed an error in locating that island to which he gives the name of Berto ; he places it three degrees more to the south east than its true position and he makes it smaller than it really is. An excusable error, if he had not seen it, but unpardonable if he landed on it on the 24th of June, 1497.

Therefore, where does that name of Breton come from? At the beginning of the sixteenth century, all the lands and islands bathed by the waters of the gulf of St. Lawrence, the largest part of which was called *Entrée des Bretons* (Entrance of the Bretons) were designated by the name of *Terres Bretonnes*, (Lands of the Bretons). The main land itself, from that part included between the French Bay (Bay of Fundy), down to the Virginia, was then called by the name of *Terre Bretonne* (Land of the Breton), and sometimes *Terre Française* (*Terra Francisca*). It can be seen on the Dauphin's map where the *Land of the Breton* is placed on this coast which was soon to be called *Norembegue*.

All was French in the surroundings, and the authorities who attribute the name of Cape Breton to the French are numerous. The English authors themselves have never sought, that I know of, to attribute the paternity of this appellation to John Cabot or to his son Sebastian. Therefore, when Cabot, in 1544, wrote his famous inscription of *Tierra prima vista*, he knew nothing of the geographical position of Cape Breton, as he took less interest in it than the Portuguese and Spanish cosmographers. How could he so perfectly describe the land he had seen for the first time, if he did not know the elementary data of the geography of that region?

37

VI

AUTHORITIES

Who are the most remarkable historians who, by their writings, do not pay any attention to Cabot's landfall at Cape Breton, and who rely on the ancient and universal belief of a landfall at Labrador or Newfoundland? Let us first quote the writers of the last centuries, those who have had the opportunity to compile the traditions and to preserve them as they were.

We have read the opinion of Ellis, an English historian of the eighteenth century. Let us listen now to Oldmixon in his work entitled : *The British Empire in America*, published in London, in 1741 :

" This large Island (Newfoundland) was discovered by Sebastian Cabot, who was sent to America by Henry VII, King of England, in the year 1497, to make Discoveries, 4 or 5 years only after Christopher Colombus had discovered the new World ".

Dumont, in his *Histoire et Commerce des Colonies Angloises*, published in London, in 1755, wrote : " Most of the English authors attribute the discovery of Newfoundland to Sebastian, although he did not take any part in it beyond accompanying his father John Cabot. It is John Cabot whom Henry VII authorized to sail, under the flag of England, for new lands. We see in Rymer's acts the patent granted to him the fifth of March, 1496 " (1).

Marvor says, in his *Historical Account of Voyages :*

" This first voyage of importance in which Sebastian Cabot was engaged, seems to have been that made by his father John, who had obtained a Commission from Henry VII for a discovery of a north west passage to India, the favourite object of Columbus. They sailed from Bristol in the spring of 1494, and pursuing their course with favouring gales, on

(1) Dumont. Histoire et Commerce des Colonies Angloises, p. 28.

the 24th of June saw Newfoundland, to which they gave the name of Prima Vista, or First Seen. Going ashore, on a small island on this Coast, they gave it the appellation of St. John's, from its being discovered on the day dedicated to St. John the Baptist. (1) "

As to the authors of the nineteenth century, we have W. Robertson who published, in 1831, an extensive work entitled : *History of the Discovery and Settlement of America*, in which he says :

" Cabot discovered a large island, which he called *Prima Vista*, and his sailors *Newfoundland;* and in a few days he descried a smaller isle, to which he gave the name of *St. John.* He landed on both these (June 24)."

In 1833, P. F. Tytler published in New York a book entitled : *Historical View of the Progress of Discovery of the more Northern Coast of America,* where we find that Cabot discovered, in 1497, "the New Isle, which was probably the name then given to Newfoundland" (2).

Let us now quote the Canadian historians, English and French. What does Garneau say :

_____

(1) Marvor. Historical account of the most celebrated Voyages, Travels, and Discoveries from the time of Columbus to the present period. *London,* 1796. 25 vol. 18mo. Vol. I, p. 67.
(2) Page 18.

" Early in 1497, Sebastian (John) Cabot, sailed in a Bristol ship with the view of seeking a N. W. passage to India. On June 24th he reached the American N. E. coast, probably the shore-line of Labrador, about lat. 56' n." (1).

Ferland writes : The 24th of June 1497, John Cabot, Venetian, and his son Sebastian, born at Bristol, England, having received a Commission from Henri VII, king of England, to go to the discovery of some new lands, sighted America near the 56th degree of north latitude " (2).

Kingsford says :

" Cabot's voyage to Newfoundland was in 1497. It was at this date the reign of Henry VII, that the first effort was made for the creation of an English navy."

We can see in McMullin : " Cabot sailed from the port of Bristol about the middle of May, 1497 ; and following very nearly the same course now pursued by vessels making the voyage from Great Britain to North America, discovered, on the 26th of June, the Island of Newfoundland, etc."

Roberts : " An expedition from Bristol, under the leadership of John Cabot, reached the continent at a point which is now Canadian territory." And he adds this note : " Pro-

(1) Garneau, translated by A. Bell. vol. I, p. 45.
(3) Ferland. Histoire du Canada, vol. I, p. 9.

bably a point on the Labrador coast, though some authorities hold it to have been the gulf coast of Nova Scotia. "

Clement in his manual of Canadian History writes : " In 1497, Henry VII commissioned a Venetian navigator, John Cabot, to sail north westerly, in the hope that in that direction perchance a way to Asia might be found. But, it has never been made quite clear what part of our coast he visited."

Among the writers of the nineteenth century, there are those to whom the discovery of Cabot's planisphere has given prudence, there are those also who have seized upon that document as if it were sure, irrefutable, worthy of faith. Among them we see celebrated men like Harrisse, Mgr Howley, S. E. Dawson, Prowse, J. P. Howley, Mgr O'Brien, Harvey, Bryant, Dr Kohl, Deane, D'Avezac, and how many others ? Each one advocates his favorite thesis. The result is that, with such a conflict of opinions, it is impossible to distinguish truth from error.

At all events we must concede, and many may be of that opinion, that Harrisse is the historian who has written the most on Cabot ; he has collected several documents and he has used them with knowledge. His last work published in the English language, in London, is the work of a man who knows the subject he is treating ; if, after this, his testimony be not worth more than that of an obscure historian, it is entirely useless to advance an opinion based on his. Let him refute this who feels able to do so. Harrisse pretends that the Cabotian map has been interpolated, for some unknown reasons, and that Sebastian Cabot is not always credible, since he has often disguised the truth, when it served his interests to do so. Cabot often contradicts himself, and he often commits some very apparent anachronisms. His map has been made out of a French map published three years previous ; as well, after all, as the whole of his cartographical work on America is modeled on the maps of which that of Cartier is the prototype.

To close this study, I do not think I can do better than to quote the opinion of two men very well known by all the historians. One is a Canadian, of Scottish descent, the other is an American ; both have made special studies on the cosmography of ancient times. Very well posted up in the matters pertaining to the history of Canada and America, they have published works of great value and of authoritative weight. One is Mr. J. G. Bourinot, secretary of the Royal Society of Canada ; the name of the other is Justin Winsor : he has been for a long time librarian of the famous University of Cambridge.

Mr. Bourinot has written a history of Cape Breton, his native country. His work is conscienciously made, full of bibliographical references. He has particularly applied his studies to thoroughly characterize the voyages of the first dis-coverers in the Gulf of St. Lawrence ; he follows them every where, and aided by documents as well as maps, his solu-tions are correct enough. In short, he is an authority for me. Well, let us quote what he says touching the question interested :

" In a map of 1544, only discovered in Germany in 1843, and attributed to Sebastian Cabot, but not accepted by all historians as authentic, the northeastern point of the main-land of North America, presumably Cape North, is put down as " prima tierra vista " ; and there are not a few historical students who believe that this was actually the landfall seen by John Cabot in his first memorable voyage to this Conti-nent. In the controversy which has gone for years as to the first land seen by Cabot and his son — whether the Coast of Labrador, or the northeastern cape of Cape Breton, or Cape Bonavista, or some other headland on the eastern shore of Newfoundland — many speculations and arguments have been, and will probably continue to be advanced in support of these various theories ; and the reader who wishes to come to some definite conclusion on this vexed subject only rises from the study of these learned disquisitions with the feeling that a great mass of knowledge has been devoted to very little purpose except that purpose be to leave the question still open, and give employment to learned antiquarians for all time to come " (1).

Justin Winsor had before him all the maps of the sixteenth century, when, after having studied them thoroughly, he has written in his book entitled *Columbus*, the following appreciation of Cabot's life and works. That distinguished historian is not more affirmative than Mr. Bourinot :

" Cabot was for over three hundred years considered as having made his landfall on the coast of Labrador, or at least we find no record that the legend of the map of 1544, placing it at Cape Breton, had impressed itself authoritatively upon the minds of Cabot's contemporaries and successors. Biddle and Humbodlt, in the early part of the present century, accepted the Labrador landfall with little question. So it happened that when, in 1843, the Cabot mappemonde of 1544 was discovered, and it was to place the landfall at the island of Cape Breton, a certain definiteness, where there have been so much vagueness, afforded the student some relief ; but as the novelty of the sensation wore off, confidence was again lost, inasmuch as the various uncertainties of the document give much ground for the rejection of all points of the testimony at variance with better vouched beliefs...

(1) Bourinot. History of Cape Breton. Transactions of Royal Society of Canada, 1891. vol. IX, p. 176 and 177.

" Here is some ground for thinking that he could not have entered the gulf of St. Lawrence at all. He landed nowhere and saw no inhabitants. If he struck the mainland, it was probably the coasts of New Brunswick or Labrador, bordering on the Gulf of Saint-Lawrence ".

www.ingramcontent.com/pod-product-compliance
Lightning Source LLC
Chambersburg PA
CDIIW032141270626
47172CB00009B/837

*9 7 8 3 3 3 7 3 9 9 2 6 9 *